The Hedgehogs' Christmas Tree

BY
KATHRYN JACKSON

ILLUSTRATED BY
AMYE ROSENBERG

GOLDEN PRESS • NEW YORK
Western Publishing Company, Inc., Racine, Wisconsin

t was Christmas Eve—at last!

Mr. Hedgehog had gone out to fetch a Christmas tree.

"He forgot the sled!" cried Mrs. Hedgehog.

"We'll take it to him," the little Hedgehogs said. "And we'll help pull the tree home, too."

"But how are we to find Daddy?" they called back.
"He went to the pine woods," answered their
mother, "so just sniff for the scent of pine."

Sniff-sniff. Was this the scent of pine?
No, it was the pear Mr. Raccoon was eating.
"Have some," he said, holding out a whole sackful.

Sniff-sniff. Was this the scent of pine?

No. It was the candy canes Mr. Mouse was taking home.

"Trade you some for a pear," he said.

Mrs. Mouse was making butterscotch icicles.
The little Hedgehogs licked the stirring spoons.
They helped with the washing up — and Mrs. Mouse
gave them a box full of golden icicles to take home.

Now the little Hedgehogs sniffed a crispy scent.
"We're making popcorn garlands," the Rabbits
called. "Come in and make some for *your* tree, too."
It was dusk when the little Hedgehogs started home.

They hurried along with their sledful of goodies.
They ran past the soft-smelling bayberry thicket.

They raced past the fresh-smelling cedar tree.

Then suddenly, they sniffed another scent....

It came from the rosemary wreath on their own door.

"You're home at last, little Hedgehogs," their mother cried, "and with such lovely things to hang on our tree!"

"But we didn't bring the tree— or Daddy!" the little Hedgehogs wailed. "We forgot all about finding our Daddy!"

"You've found me now," said Mr. Hedgehog, hurrying out.

He scooped up those little Hedgehogs and carried them into their warm, snug house.

It was filled with a wonderful Christmasy scent.

For there stood a tall, most beautiful pine tree.

"How did it GET here?" the little Hedgehogs gasped.

"On my big strong shoulder," chuckled Mr. Hedgehog and, in a wink, all the Hedgehogs were trimming their tree with pears, candy canes, popcorn garlands, golden icicles and, at the top, one single, shining star.